For Papa, who always has a story
—R.D.S.

To H$_2$O
—B.S.

Farrar Straus Giroux Books for Young Readers
175 Fifth Avenue, New York 10010

Text copyright © 2016 by Randall de Sève
Pictures copyright © 2016 by Bob Staake
All rights reserved
Printed in China by Macmillan Production (Asia) Ltd.,
Kowloon Bay, Hong Kong (supplier code PS)
Designed by Andrew Arnold
First edition, 2016
1 3 5 7 9 10 8 6 4 2

mackids.com

Library of Congress Cataloging-in-Publication Data

Names: De Sève, Randall, author. | Staake, Bob, 1957– illustrator.
Title: A fire truck named Red / Randall de Sève ; pictures by Bob Staake.
Description: First edition. | New York : Farrar Straus Giroux, 2015. |
    Summary: "A young boy has his heart set on a brand-new toy fire truck, so he is disappointed when he gets
    his grandfather's rusty old fire truck, Red, instead. But working together, the boy and his grandfather patch
    Red right up while Grandpa tells his grandson all about the adventures he had with Red when he was a boy"—
    Provided by publisher.
Identifiers: LCCN 2015030358 | ISBN 9780374300739 (hardback)
Subjects: | CYAC: Fire engines—Fiction. | Toys—Fiction. | Grandfathers—Fiction. | Grandparent and child—
    Fiction. | BISAC: JUVENILE FICTION / Transportation / Cars & Trucks. | JUVENILE FICTION / Family /
    Multigenerational. | JUVENILE FICTION / Toys, Dolls, Puppets. | JUVENILE FICTION / Boys & Men.
Classification: LCC PZ7.D4504 Fi 2015 | DDC [E]—dc23
LC record available at http://lccn.loc.gov/2015030358

Our books may be purchased in bulk for promotional, educational, or business use. Please contact your local bookseller or the Macmillan
Corporate and Premium Sales Department at (800) 221-7945 ext. 5442 or by e-mail at MacmillanSpecialMarkets@macmillan.com.

A FIRE TRUCK NAMED

RED

RANDALL DE SÈVE   *Pictures by* BOB STAAKE

Farrar Straus Giroux
New York

This is the shiny new fire truck Rowan wanted for his birthday:

It has a ladder that reaches
all the way up

and a hose that sprays real water.

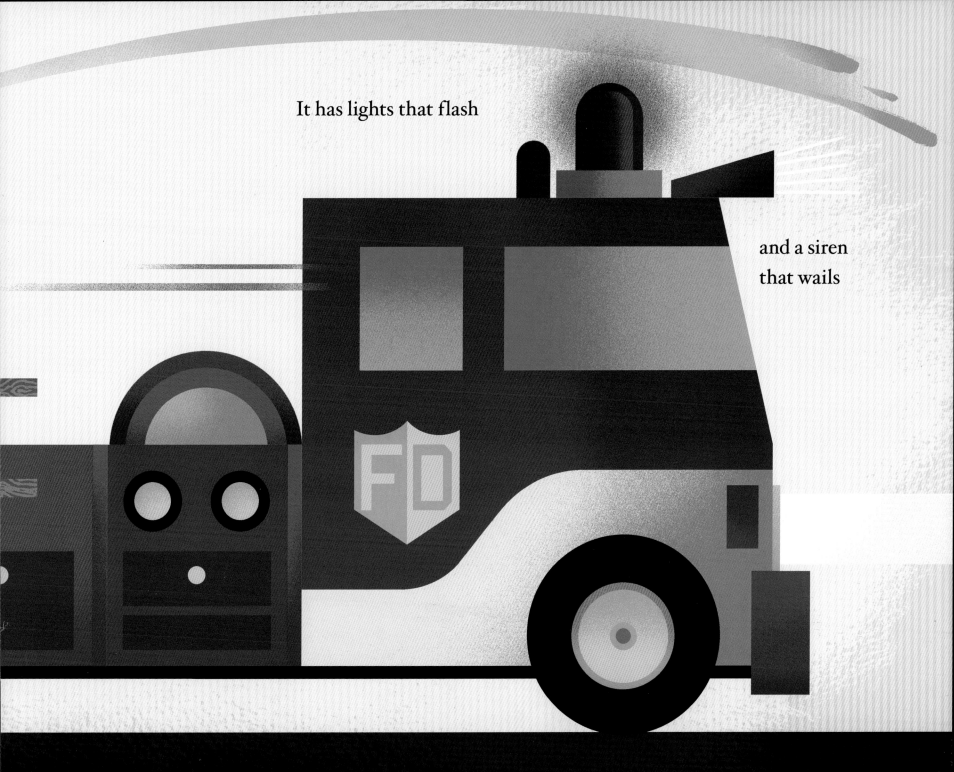

It has lights that flash

and a siren that wails

and wheels that spin, silent and smooth.

"It was mine when I was a boy," his grandfather said.
"No blaze was too big, no rescue too small for Red and me."

But Rowan barely heard his papa.
He was busy trying not to cry.

"Trust me, Ro," said Papa with a wink.
"We'll fix up Red *better* than new."

That afternoon, Papa and Rowan got to work.

"Red and I were a great team.
Our very first day,
we got called to rescue a cat
from the top of a tall oak tree."

Rowan looked over at Papa's cat, Fritz.
Cats are boring, he thought.
Still, he knew how to be polite.
"So what did you do?"

"Red and I rushed to the scene!

"Red's ladder reached all the way up— and we got that scared cat down. Poor thing kicked and clawed the whole way. That cat was nearly as strong as the elephants."

"Elephants?"
Rowan *loved* elephants.

"Oh yes. Later that morning, Red and I got called by the circus.
It was very hot in the tent, and they had run out of water.
The elephants were thirsty, and they needed a bath."

"Elephants do need water," Rowan agreed.
"So what did you do?"

"Red and I rushed to the scene!
We hosed down those elephants.
And those elephants were so happy . . . they hosed *us* back!

"We hosed until the water ran out. Then we returned to the station to refill Red's tanks—and good thing we did, because a big blaze broke out in the library that very afternoon!"

"Good thing!" Rowan echoed.
"So what did you do?"

"Red and I rushed to the scene!
We raced up and down steep hills,
lights flashing,
siren wailing!

"Fog rolled in, thick as a milkshake,
but Red saw right through it.

"Cars crawled along, slow as snails, but Red raced right past them. Those old roads were bumpy—but Red's ride was smooth."

Weeeeeeeeee

Now Rowan could hear Red's siren.
He could see Red's lights,
the fog,
the traffic.

He helped oil Red's wheels: *smooth*.

"The library was smoking when we got there," Papa continued. "Heat peeled the paint right off Red's nose— but that didn't stop us.

"We doused that fire
and saved the books!
Most of them, at least."

"We sure did!" yelled Rowan.

And then he took a good
long look at Red.

Even with shiny fresh paint,
wheels that spin,
a hose that sprays,
and a ladder that reaches all the way up,
Red would never be new.
But . . .

We could be a great team,
Rowan thought.

And they were.

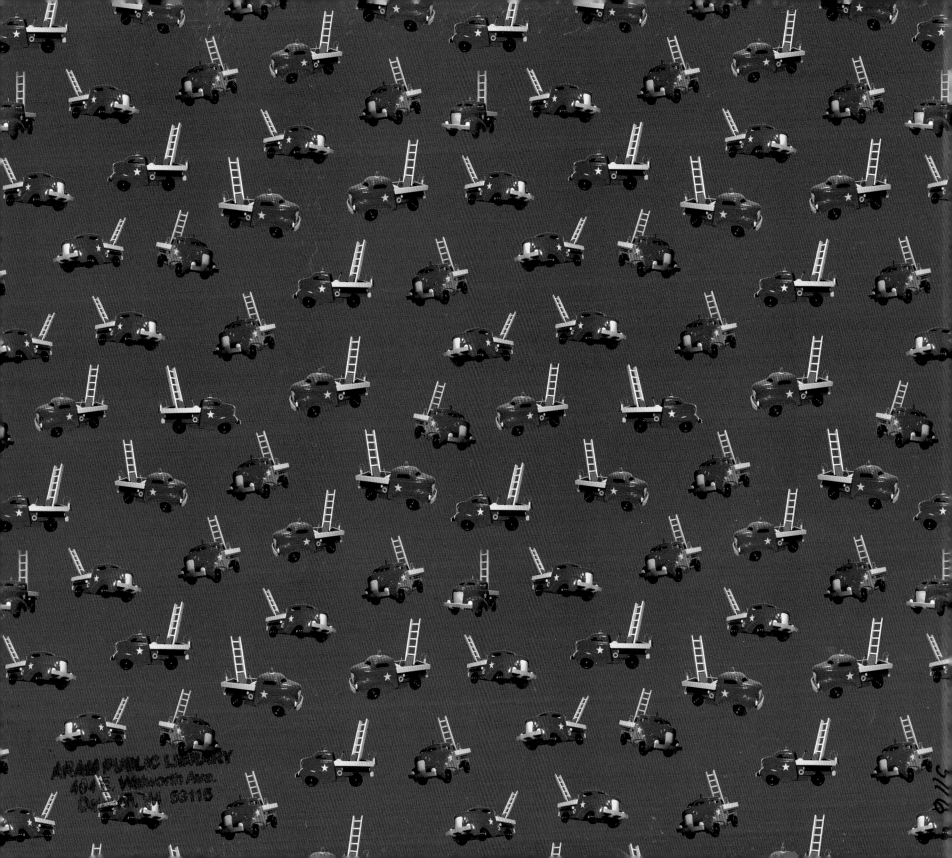